To: ....

From: ....

GROSSET & DUNLAP
Penguin Young Readers Group
An Imprint of Penguin Random House LLC

All rights reserved. Previously published in 2017 by Egmont UK Limited
as *My Mummy*. Published in the United States of America in 2019 by Grosset & Dunlap,
an imprint of Penguin Random House LLC, 345 Hudson Street, New York, New York 10014.
GROSSET & DUNLAP is a trademark of Penguin Random House LLC. Manufactured in China.

www.mrmen.com

The publisher does not have any control over and does not assume any
responsibility for author or third-party websites or their content.

ISBN 9781524792381   10 9 8 7 6 5 4 3 2 1

MY MOM
and me
by Roger Hargreaves

Grosset & Dunlap
An Imprint of Penguin Random House

My mom brightens my day from the moment she wakes up.

She is like Little Miss Sunshine on a cloudy day.

My mom can do more than one thing at a time, like magic.

And when she reads
me stories, I feel like
I'm really there.

My mom is very friendly and likes to talk to people.

But she is also good at listening, especially to me.

My mom is curious and sometimes asks lots of questions.

But she is also wise and knows lots of answers.

My mom knows when I am hungry...

. . .and when I am tired.
. : . .and when I am tired.

My mom can be very silly and always makes
me smile.

She gives the best hugs
and knows just when they
are needed.

My mom has
a splendid sense
of style.

And she has lots of interesting things stored in mysterious boxes.

My mom loves eating cake, just like me.

And sometimes she needs time to herself, too.

My mom can be a bit mischievous.

But she is always kind.

My mom is lots of fun
and loves birthday parties.

She is really good at playing games like hide-and-seek.

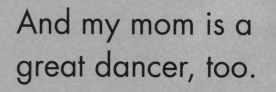

And my mom is a
great dancer, too.

Even when things go wrong, my mom makes me smile.

When she giggles, it makes me giggle, too.

And when I make my mom happy, she jumps for joy!

There is no one like my mom, though sometimes I wish there were two of her.

My mom is SO very special. My mom loves me, and I love my mom.

MY MOM

My mom is most like **LITTLE MISS** ....

I love it when my mom reads ....

.... to me.

My mom makes me laugh when ....

....

She always knows when ....

....

My mom is very kind because ....

....

My mom is lots of fun and likes ....

Her favorite game to play with me is ....

I know she loves me when ....

My mom's hugs are the best because ....

....

This is a picture
of my mom:

by ....

age ....